The Layers Between Us

OrangeBooks Publication

1st Floor, Rajhans Arcade, Mall Road, Kohka, Bhilai, Chhattisgarh 490020
Website: **www.orangebooks.in**

First Edition, 2025

ISBN: 978-93-7426-060-9

Price: Rs. 249.00

Printed in India

THE LAYERS Between us

Love, Attention, and Consciousness Amid the Illusion of Separation

Mohan Krishna

OrangeBooks Publication
www.orangebooks.in

Author's Note

This book does not argue for a belief system, nor does it attempt to explain reality.

What follows is a record of lived experience—of attention, fear, love, imagination, and moments that resisted easy interpretation. Some events described here may appear coincidental, symbolic, or ambiguous. They are presented as they were experienced, without asking the reader to accept any conclusion beyond what the experience itself offers.

I have tried to write with restraint. Not to persuade, but to observe. Not to explain consciousness, but to describe how it is encountered in ordinary life—through silence, relationship, memory, and questioning.

Readers trained in science may find uncertainty where they expect evidence. Readers drawn to spirituality may find hesitation where they expect certainty. This is intentional. The book exists in that middle space, where meaning arises not from answers, but from sustained attention.

If there is a single invitation here, it is this:

to read without urgency,

to allow ambiguity,

and to notice what arises when experience is taken seriously—without being forced into belief.

Contents

Chapter - 1
The Child Who Watched Himself

He learned fear before he learned language.

It did not arrive as a single event, but as a quiet accumulation—small moments that taught him to observe himself from the outside. When he entered a room, his attention did not move outward to the faces, the walls, or the sounds. It folded inward, asking a single, persistent question:

What do they think of me?

The question became a habit.

The habit became a lens.

And through that lens, the world appeared sharp, judgmental, and slightly dangerous.

As a child, he believed everyone was watching him as closely as he watched himself. A laugh across the room felt directed. A whisper became evidence. Silence was never neutral; it meant something had already been decided.

In reality, no one was paying such attention. Each person carried their own private weather of thoughts, fears, and distractions. But this was invisible to him then. His inner world spoke louder than the outer one.

School amplified the condition. Classrooms, with their rows and routines, became theatres of exposure. When the teacher asked a question, his body tightened before his mind could respond. His heart raced ahead of his thoughts. Even when he knew the answer, fear arrived first.

Some children noticed the hesitation. They did not understand it, but they recognised vulnerability when they saw it. Teasing began casually—glances, comments, imitations. Nothing dramatic. Nothing that could be reported. Just enough to confirm what he already believed:

Being seen was unsafe.

So, he learned to disappear.

He spoke less. He laughed quietly. He stayed inside—both physically and mentally. While others ran, argued, and claimed space, he withdrew into observation. He watched people the way one watches passing trains: with curiosity, distance, and the sense that they were going somewhere he was not.

This inwardness had a consequence.

Because he spent so much time watching himself, he also became skilled at watching others. He noticed tone shifts, pauses, and expressions that escaped language. He sensed emotions before they were named. What he lacked in confidence, he compensated for in perception.

But perception without grounding can turn inward and become surveillance.

By adolescence, the habit was deeply installed. His body reacted before his mind. Fear did not announce itself; it simply shaped his decisions.

At thirteen, something unfamiliar entered his life.

It did not come as certainty or courage. It came quietly, like recognition.

There was a girl.

She was not dramatic. Not loud. Not impossibly distant. She existed within the ordinary rhythms of school life, which made the feeling harder to name. When he saw her, nothing exploded. Instead, something aligned. The world did not stop—but it softened.

He did not know the word *love*. What he knew was attention without effort. His thoughts returned to her without being summoned. When she smiled, it did not register as approval, but as warmth.

He never spoke to her about it.

Silence, by then, was not a choice. It was structured.

What he could not know at that age was that attention often moves both ways. She noticed him too—quietly, without announcement. In the same way he observed the world, she observed him.

A dance program was approaching.

She wanted to tell him which song she would dance to. The intention appeared more than once, then retreated. Each time, the moment passed. Words remained suspended between hesitation and timing.

He, meanwhile, imagined.

Without knowing the song, his mind constructed one. He dreamed of the performance—not deliberately, not symbolically, but as the mind does when it fills an absence. In the dream, there was a specific song. A particular rhythm. A feeling of familiarity without explanation.

He did not tell anyone.

When the day of the performance arrived, he watched from his seat with the usual distance—until the music began.

It was the same song.

Not similar. Not close.

The same.

Something in him went still. Not excitement. Not fear. Just a brief suspension, as if the mind had lost its footing. He did not interpret it. He did not explain it. At thirteen, he did not yet have the language for coincidence, intuition, or probability.

He only knew that something imagined had quietly crossed into reality.

Years later, he would understand something he did not then: dreams are not predictions. They are rehearsals for meaning.

Life continued, indifferent to inner realisations.

She changed schools.

There was no dramatic goodbye. No final conversation. Just absence, arriving quietly and staying.

What remained was not regret, but incompletion—a sense that something had begun without instruction on how to end.

He did not yet know how often this pattern would repeat.

What he knew was this: some experiences do not wound because they hurt, but because they remain unfinished.

And so, the child who watched himself continued growing—carrying silence like a second spine—unaware that observation itself would one day become both his prison and his path.

Chapter - 2
The Shape of Unspoken Things

Adolescence did not arrive as transformation. It arrived as pressure.

His body began changing before his inner architecture knew how to accommodate it. Growth brought attention, and attention intensified the habit of self-monitoring. Where others experimented loudly—with clothes, friendships, defiance—he refined invisibility.

Silence, however, is never empty. It accumulates content.

Thoughts multiplied in the absence of speech. Imagined conversations replaced real ones. He rehearsed sentences he would never say, refining tone and timing for moments that did not arrive. What appeared externally as withdrawal was, internally, constant motion.

The girl from school did not disappear from his mind when she left. She changed form.

She became less a person and more a symbol—not idealised, but suspended. In his memory, she represented a moment when the world had felt briefly possible. He did not long for her specifically. He longed for the version of himself that had existed in her presence.

This distinction mattered, though he would not recognise it for years.

Imagination expanded to fill emotional gaps. Music became a private language. Certain songs felt inhabited, as though they contained rooms he could enter and stay. When he listened, his body softened. Attention loosened its grip. For short periods, he forgot to watch himself.

These moments were rare, but instructive.

He noticed that when attention relaxed, fear receded. Not because anything had changed externally, but because the internal observer had stepped back.

School continued. Expectations accumulated. Comparisons multiplied. He noticed differences—between wealth and scarcity, confidence and hesitation, visibility and neglect. These distinctions did not yet feel political or philosophical. They felt personal, as though the world had been unevenly distributed.

He learned early that some children moved through space as if entitled to it. Others asked permission with every step. He belonged to the latter category.

This awareness hardened into a quiet resentment—not toward people, but toward circumstance. He did not want what others had. He wanted to understand why experience itself seemed unequally weighted.

Questions began forming beneath conscious thought.

Why did some voices carry authority before they spoke?

Why did fear feel inherited?

Why did silence feel safer than expression, even when it hurt?

These were not articulated questions. They existed as tensions in the body.

When he reached college age, physical distance provided a new illusion: that environment alone might resolve what psychology could not. A different city, different faces, different rhythms. Perhaps the observer would finally rest.

It did not.

The habit travelled intact.

What changed, however, was exposure.

During his first year, a friend invited him to a birthday celebration in another city. The invitation felt risky—not because of danger, but because of proximity. New people meant new mirrors.

Before the party, they gathered at a friend's house.

The house belonged to a girl whose parents were unaware of the gathering. This secrecy introduced a shared tension that softened individual differences. Everyone moved carefully, voices lowered, laughter restrained. A small room upstairs became their temporary refuge.

There were eight of them—four boys, four girls—sitting close, shoulders nearly touching.

Someone suggested ghost stories.

The suggestion was childish, but effective. Fear redistributed attention outward. For the first time that evening, his awareness left him.

Then one of the girls cried out.

She said she had seen something at the window.

The room froze.

He did not think. He acted.

A pillow lay beside him. He passed it to her without explanation, a simple gesture, instinctive and uncalculated. The movement surprised him as much as anyone else.

When he looked up, their eyes met.

Nothing dramatic occurred.

There was no certainty, no revelation, no rush of narrative meaning. There was only recognition—a quiet, bodily knowing that bypassed thought.

Later, he would try to explain this moment. He would fail.

What he knew then was limited but precise: attention had landed somewhere outside itself.

Fear retreated.

He did not speak to her that night beyond necessary politeness. Words returned too slowly. But something had already shifted. The observer had loosened its grip, if only briefly.

This, too, became a pattern.

He would feel deeply. He would not act.

Inaction, over time, does not remain neutral. It transforms into attachment.

Years passed.

He carried her presence quietly through them—not as obsession, but as continuity. She represented a moment when he had responded without fear. That mattered more than romance.

Nine years later, he saw her again at a friend's wedding.

She stood across the room, familiar and distant, embedded in a different life. The context made conversation possible. The moment invited closure.

He did not move.

The internal calculation was immediate and merciless: *If I speak and fail, the image collapses. If I remain silent, it survives.*

He chose survival.

Afterwards, the cost revealed itself.

Silence, once protective, began to feel corrosive.

The observer returned, harsher than before.

And slowly, without ceremony, the weight accumulated.

What he had not yet learned was this: avoiding pain does not prevent it. It only delays its instruction.

The lesson was approaching.

Chapter - 3
When Silence Turned Heavy

Silence had once been a shelter.

For years, it protected him from exposure, from error, from the unpredictable reactions of others. But shelters, when lived in too long, become confinements.

After the wedding, something shifted. Not abruptly, not visibly. The change arrived as weight.

Mornings grew slower. Decisions that once required little effort—getting up, answering messages, entering rooms—began to demand negotiation. His body moved, but without momentum, as though gravity had subtly increased.

This was not sadness in the dramatic sense. There were no tears, no clear despair. What he experienced was dullness—an emotional flattening that made everything feel slightly distant. Pleasure did not disappear; it became muted. Pain did not announce itself; it lingered.

Isolation, once chosen, now imposed itself.

He began spending more time alone. Not in solitude, which can be nourishing, but in withdrawal. Rooms felt safer than people. Silence became dense, filled with unfinished thoughts.

During this period, he became acutely aware of the difference.

It appeared first in ordinary settings—classrooms, streets, public spaces. He noticed how some people spoke without hesitation, their voices carrying an assumed legitimacy. Others measured every word, adjusting posture and tone as if anticipating correction.

He began to see patterns.

Money influenced ease. Language influenced authority. Clothing influenced attention. These observations were not theoretical; they were visceral. He felt them in his body—how shoulders tightened in certain rooms, how breath shortened in others.

The world began to resemble a structure layered with invisible partitions.

Rich and poor.

Confident and cautious.

Visible and overlooked.

These divisions were rarely spoken of, yet constantly enforced.

He did not interpret this as injustice in a political sense. It felt more existential. As though reality itself had been stratified, distributing experience unevenly.

At times, this awareness sharpened into resentment. Not toward individuals, but toward the mechanisms that seemed to shape human interaction before intention could intervene.

Why did some lives feel lighter?

Why did others carry friction?

He had no answers. Only accumulation.

The accumulation eventually demanded expression.

One evening, alone, the thought arrived uninvited: *What if the distance between people is not natural, but constructed?*

The idea did not feel revolutionary. It felt obvious, as though it had always been present but unnamed.

If divisions were learned, they could also be unlearned.

This thought unsettled him.

Because if separation was not inevitable, then silence was not neutral. Withdrawal was not harmless. Avoidance was participation.

The observer—his long-standing internal companion—turned its gaze outward.

He began noticing how often people spoke past one another. How quickly identity solidified around labels: profession, status, origin. How easily complexity collapsed into categories.

The more he observed, the more artificial these boundaries appeared.

At the same time, a parallel awareness emerged—one less conceptual, more sensory.

Nature began asserting itself in his perception.

Not as beauty, not as escape, but as contrast.

He noticed how trees occupied space without apology. How rivers did not negotiate their direction. How birds did not compare themselves mid-flight.

This was not romanticisation. It was an observation.

The natural world appeared indifferent to human hierarchies.

During periods of environmental disruption—floods, storms, news of distant calamities—he felt an unexpected internal resonance. Not fear, but recognition. As though the external disorder mirrored an internal one.

A question formed, tentative and unresolved:

What if division itself creates instability?

He did not know whether this was a metaphor or a mechanism.

What he knew was experiential: separation felt tense; moments of shared humanity felt easing.

At times, this awareness overwhelmed him. The sense of fragmentation—within society, within himself—felt too large to reconcile.

He did not try to fix it.

Instead, he retreated further.

Depression, when quiet, often masquerades as thoughtfulness. He mistook inertia for contemplation. Days passed without distinction. Time flattened.

Yet beneath the stagnation, something reorganised.

The observer, exhausted by self-surveillance, began to question its own role.

What if attention itself was shaping experience?

This was not yet insight. It was a pressure point.

Something was preparing to shift.

He did not know what form it would take. He only sensed that the old way—watching, withdrawing, enduring had reached its limit.

Silence, once a refuge, had become a question.

And questions, he would soon learn, do not remain unanswered forever.

Chapter - 4
The Day the Layers Became Visible

The change did not announce itself.

There was no moment of anticipation, no heightened emotion that signaled importance. The day unfolded like any other—ordinary, unmarked, resistant to memory. What distinguished it revealed itself only afterward.

He was walking alone, moving without destination. This had become habitual: motion without purpose, thinking without direction. The city moved around him in fragments—conversations half-heard, vehicles passing, faces appearing and vanishing.

Then, without warning, perception altered.

It was not visual in the cinematic sense. The streets did not glow. Objects did not blur. What changed was relational.

People no longer appeared as individuals first.

They appeared as positions.

Layers became visible—not literally, but unmistakably. Each person seemed situated within an invisible structure, separated by subtle partitions. These partitions were not physical, yet they exerted force.

Status. Identity. Expectation.

They hovered between bodies, shaping interaction before words could intervene.

He stopped walking.

The experience carried no fear. Instead, there was a strange neutrality, as though emotion had stepped aside to allow observation.

He noticed how rarely people met each other directly. How often did communication occur through roles rather than presence? A shopkeeper spoke from habit. A customer responded from an assumption. An official addressed a category, not a person.

These patterns had existed before. What changed was clarity.

The divisions appeared learned, reinforced, repeated—so embedded they masqueraded as nature.

In this perception, conflict made sense.

Not as malice, but as friction.

Friction was created wherever separation hardened.

As this understanding deepened, another association arose, uninvited.

Images of environmental disruption surfaced—flooded streets, cracked earth, displaced lives. He did not interpret these as punishment or a message. They appeared as parallel phenomena: systems under strain.

What if instability, whether social or environmental, followed similar dynamics?

The thought unsettled him.

Because it suggested participation.

If division contributed to tension, then every act of separation—internal or external—added pressure. Withdrawal was not neutral. Silence had consequences.

The realisation did not carry blame. It carried responsibility.

He noticed his own position within the layers.

He was neither central nor peripheral, neither powerful nor invisible. He occupied a middle space—observing without intervening.

For the first time, this stance felt insufficient.

The observer recognised its own limit.

The experience lasted minutes, perhaps seconds. Time felt irrelevant. When it receded, the world returned unchanged. People continued walking. Conversations resumed their usual cadence.

Yet something irreversible had occurred.

He could no longer pretend the layers were imagined.

At the same time, certainty did not follow.

Was this insight, or projection?

Was he perceiving structure, or constructing it?

He held both possibilities without resolution.

What mattered was effect.

From that day forward, he could not unsee the space between people. He noticed how quickly unity was spoken of, and how rarely embodied. How often are ideals replaced contact?

This awareness did not make him hopeful.

It made him careful.

If unity were to exist, it would not arrive as ideology. It would have to be practised internally, where separation first takes root.

He did not join movements. He did not preach. He did not explain.

He began, instead, with attention.

When fear arose, he noticed it without retreat.

When judgment surfaced, he traced its origin.

When silence appeared, he questioned its function.

This was not activism.

It was an experiment.

And like all experiments, it introduced uncertainty.

He had crossed a threshold without knowing its destination.

What lay ahead was not clarity, but inquiry.

And inquiry, once genuine, refuses to remain contained.

Chapter - 5
Territories of the Mind

After the day the layers became visible, his attention no longer moved automatically.

Thoughts still arose, but they no longer felt identical to him. A small distance appeared between awareness and content. This distance was not constant; it flickered. But once noticed, it could not be forgotten.

Sleep began to change.

Dreams, once scattered and forgettable, grew vivid. Not dramatic, not symbolic in obvious ways—simply coherent. They possessed continuity, as though occurring in a space governed by its own logic.

He did not search for meaning.

At first, he only noticed the terrain.

Some dreams unfolded like landscapes. Others resembled rooms—enclosed, precise, almost architectural. Some corridors led nowhere, thresholds that invited crossing, and spaces that felt familiar without memory.

On waking, he felt neither inspired nor disturbed. He felt oriented.

The contrast between waking and dreaming softened. Boundaries blurred, not in content but in quality. Attention carried the same texture in both states: quiet, receptive, less urgent.

He began reading.

Not systematically. Not devotionally. He read fragments—psychology, philosophy, neuroscience, and personal accounts. The material mattered less than the posture it suggested: observation without immediate explanation.

One idea returned repeatedly across disciplines—that consciousness is not a thing, but a field of activity. That experience depends less on what appears than on how it is attended to.

This resonated, but he did not adopt it.

He had learned caution.

Patterns invite belief. Belief hardens perception.

Instead, he experimented.

He noticed how thought altered sensation. How anticipation tightened the body. How memory colored the present. He noticed how fear accelerated time, and how stillness expanded it.

These observations were subtle, but cumulative.

One night, a dream arrived with unusual clarity.

He was walking through a place that felt both unfamiliar and precise. The air carried weight. Movement required intention. In the dream, he met a woman.

There was nothing extraordinary about her appearance. What distinguished the encounter was recognition—not emotional, not romantic. Structural.

As though two coordinates had aligned.

They spoke briefly. Numbers surfaced in the exchange, without emphasis. They did not feel symbolic. They felt incidental.

He woke without interpretation.

Weeks later, circumstances brought him into contact with a woman whose presence echoed the dream—not in detail, but in pattern. The resemblance unsettled him.

He noticed the mind's tendency to connect.

Coincidence, once noticed, amplifies itself.

Still, he did not dismiss the experience. He held it lightly, as one holds a fragile object—careful not to squeeze meaning into it.

When he spoke to her, his voice did not retreat.

This surprised him.

He expressed interest plainly, without rehearsal. The response was clear and kind, but negative.

Rejection arrived without collapse.

What followed was unexpected.

Thought quieted.

For a brief interval, the observer vanished.

There was no analysis, no internal narration. Sensation remained, but interpretation did not. He felt present without reference.

The state did not last.

But it left residue.

He recognised it later in moments of absorption—in listening, in walking, in silence. A condition without commentary.

This experience unsettled his assumptions.

If thought could pause without effort, then identity was not continuous. If identity were not continuous, then much of what he feared was optional.

Another dream followed months later.

Another encounter, similarly aligned.

This time, the woman was married.

There was no pursuit, no confusion. Only recognition of pattern, followed by release.

He, spoke of these experiences cautiously.

Some listened with curiosity. Others responded with humour or dismissal. Laughter did not wound him as it once would have. He noticed the reflex to explain away what unsettled shared assumptions.

He did not argue.

He had learned that experience does not require validation.

What mattered was function.

Dreams had become territories—not messages, not prophecies, but environments where attention trained itself differently. Waking life now contained similar thresholds.

He began to suspect that consciousness does not expand by acquiring content, but by relinquishing fixation.

This suspicion did not feel final.

It felt provisional.

And provisionally, he continued.

Chapter - 6
Learning to Stay

The most difficult change was not learning something new.

It was staying.

For most of his life, attention had moved away at the first sign of discomfort. Fear initiated withdrawal. Silence served as exit. The body complied automatically, as though retreat were a reflex inherited rather than chosen.

After the experiences with dreams and the brief suspension of thought, this reflex became visible.

Visibility altered possibility.

He began noticing the moment just before departure—the tightening in the chest, the shallow breath, the impulse to disengage. Previously, these signals triggered movement. Now, they became invitations to pause.

Staying did not feel courageous.

It felt awkward.

In conversations, he resisted the urge to rehearse responses internally. He allowed gaps to remain unfilled. Silence stretched, sometimes uncomfortably. Others spoke into it, or did not. Either way, he remained present.

The body responded slowly at first.

Muscles softened where they once braced. Breathing deepened without instruction—sensations—pressure, warmth, vibration—registered without interpretation.

This was an embodiment, though he did not name it.

He learned it through error.

At times, staying in intense discomfort. Emotions surfaced that had been previously avoided—envy, grief, longing, irritation. None was dramatic. They appeared as textures rather than stories.

The mind attempted to organise them into a narrative. He noticed this tendency and declined it.

Declining narrative did not eliminate experience.

It clarified it.

In this clarity, innocence reappeared—not as naivety, but as immediacy. Experience met awareness without mediation. The world did not need to be improved to be encountered.

He observed children differently.

Their attention moved fluidly. They responded fully, then released. Emotion did not linger as identity. Watching them, he recognised a capacity that adulthood often obscures: the ability to inhabit the present without commentary.

This recognition did not romanticise childhood.

It contextualised it.

Education, he realised, shapes attention as much as knowledge. What is emphasised becomes central; what is ignored recedes into the background. Patterns of thought solidify early, then operate invisibly.

Trauma, too, organises awareness.

Certain experiences elevate vigilance. They place the individual on a pedestal of alertness—always watching, rarely resting. From this position, the connection feels risky.

Understanding this softened his self-judgment.

Patterns were not failures. They were adaptations.

If they could be learned, they could be reconfigured.

Staying became a practice.

In public spaces, he noticed his feet against the ground. In moments of conflict, he tracked breath before thought. In solitude, he allowed stillness without filling it.

The higher self, when it appeared, did not instruct.

It expected generosity.

Not performative giving, not sacrifice—but availability. Presence without agenda. Attention offered without demand.

He noticed that when attention was given freely, respect followed indirectly. When respect diminished, it often pointed to undeveloped internal territory rather than external rejection.

This insight was uncomfortable.

It implied responsibility.

Rather than correcting the world, the work was internal: to meet experience fully, without escape. To stay with sensation, thought, and emotion long enough for them to resolve naturally.

Staying revealed something unexpected.

Silence was not absence.

It was coherence.

In moments of quiet presence, fragmentation eased. The body aligned. Thought slowed. The layers he once perceived between people felt less rigid—not because they vanished, but because attention no longer reinforced them.

Unity, he began to suspect, is not an idea to be adopted.

It is a condition that emerges when separation is not continually rehearsed.

This understanding did not conclude anything.

It stabilised him.

Learning to stay did not make life easier.

It made it inhabitable.

Chapter - 7
Imagination is Not Escape

For a long time, imagination had been misunderstood.

In his early years, it functioned as refuge. When the external world felt hostile or overwhelming, the mind produced alternatives—scenes, dialogues, possibilities that required no permission. This capacity had protected him, but it had also delayed engagement.

Now, imagination began to change its posture.

It no longer pulled him away from experience. It moved closer to it.

He noticed that imagination was not opposed to reality. It was a mode of exploration. Scientists used it when forming hypotheses. Artists relied on it to perceive what had not yet taken form. Children exercised it naturally, without mistaking it for fact.

The problem was not imagination.

The problem was confusion between image and belief.

When imagination hardened into conclusion, it became delusion. When it remained flexible, it became intelligent.

This distinction mattered.

He encountered ideas circulating widely—claims that humans use only a small fraction of their brains, that other beings operate at higher percentages, that imagination itself is proof of hidden capacity. These notions were attractive. They offered hierarchy, progress, and destiny.

He resisted them.

Not because imagination was weak, but because exaggeration weakened credibility.

What neuroscience actually suggested was more subtle: the brain does not operate by percentage. It operates by networks, context, and efficiency. Different states recruit different patterns. Nothing mystical was required to explain this.

This understanding did not diminish wonder.

It refined it.

Imagination, seen clearly, was not about accessing unused regions. It was about recombining what was already present in novel ways. Creativity emerged not from excess capacity, but from loosened constraint.

In this sense, imagination was disciplined freedom.

He noticed how geniuses across fields described similar processes. They spoke less of brilliance and more of curiosity. Less of answers and more questions held open long enough for something unexpected to appear.

Imagination, then, was not an escape from reality.

It was intimacy with possibility.

This reframing allowed him to revisit his own experiences without inflation. Dreams were not messages from elsewhere. They were simulations—safe environments where attention could move without consequence. Altered states were not superior realities. There were shifts in organisation.

What mattered was integration.

Could insights survive ordinary life?

If an idea dissolved under pressure, it was decoration. If it reorganised behaviour quietly, it was useful.

He tested this standard relentlessly.

The imagination that increased humility stayed.

Imagination that demanded belief was released.

This discipline protected him.

It allowed him to speak across differences without insisting on agreement. To converse with sceptics without defensiveness. To remain curious without becoming ungrounded.

In this posture, imagination regained innocence.

It became a tool for inquiry, not identity.

He began to understand that intelligence is not the accumulation of concepts, but the ability to hold complexity without rushing to closure.

This capacity, more than any theory, connected people across domains.

Scientists, artists, spiritual practitioners—all depended on the same faculty: sustained curiosity.

Imagination, when honest, served that curiosity.

And when curiosity remained alive, consciousness continued to reorganize itself—quietly, without announcement.

Chapter - 8
The Practice of One Consciousness

Unity did not arrive as belief.

If it had, he would have rejected it. Beliefs asked for allegiance. What he was discovering required participation.

The phrase *one consciousness* appeared gradually in his thinking, not as a doctrine but as shorthand. It was named an intuition that had grown through observation: separation was enacted moment by moment, and so was coherence.

Practice began where it always had—in ordinary situations.

At a shop counter, he noticed the impulse to hurry the exchange. He slowed instead, allowing eye contact without demand. The interaction changed subtly. Nothing dramatic occurred. The atmosphere softened.

On public transport, he observed irritation arise when space felt invaded. Rather than withdraw, he stayed with sensation. The irritation dissolved without a story.

These moments were small, almost forgettable. But repetition revealed a pattern.

Attention organised experience.

When attention is fixated on difference, difference is amplified. When attention rested without comparison, commonality surfaced—not as sentiment, but as shared presence.

This did not erase boundaries.

Roles remained. Context mattered. Power dynamics did not vanish. What changed was the internal rehearsal of separation. He noticed how often identity sought reinforcement through contrast.

I am not like them.

The thought appeared frequently.

He learned to treat it as a signal rather than the truth.

Giving, in this context, required redefinition.

It was not generosity as performance. It was not a sacrifice. It was availability—attention offered without strategy. Listening without planning a response. Acting without internal narration.

He noticed that when giving occurred this way, outcomes were unpredictable. Sometimes it invited connection. Sometimes it changed nothing externally.

Both were acceptable.

The practice was internal.

He also noticed resistance.

Old patterns returned under stress. Fatigue narrowed awareness. Fear reasserted hierarchy. The mind searched for certainty, for position.

This did not invalidate the practice.

It clarified its necessity.

One consciousness, he realised, was not a permanent state. It was a recurrent alignment—entered, exited, reentered. The expectation of constancy belonged to idealism. Reality moved in cycles.

Importantly, this practice did not require agreement.

He could sit with someone who denied its premise entirely and still practice it. Unity was not a consensus. It was a contact without an agenda.

This insight altered how he viewed conflict.

Disagreement did not threaten coherence. Avoidance did.

When dialogue remained present, even tension carried information. When attention withdrew, misunderstanding calcified.

He began to see social division less as moral failure and more as attentional habit.

Habits could be interrupted.

Not by force, but by noticing.

The practice extended inward.

When shame surfaced, he met it without justification. When pride appeared, he noticed the contraction it produced. When loneliness arose, he allowed it without narrative.

This internal honesty prevented projection.

The layers he once perceived between people thinned—not because society changed, but because his participation in separation decreased.

This did not makc him cxccptional.

It made him accountable.

One consciousness, practised this way, did not promise harmony. It offered clarity. From clarity, appropriate action sometimes follows. Sometimes, stillness was sufficient.

He did not frame this as a solution.

It was orientation.

And orientation, he discovered, quietly reorganises everything it touches.

Chapter - 9
When Love Reappears Without a Face

Love returned without announcement.

There was no image attached to it. No memory demanded attention. It arrived as a sensation first—a warmth without direction, a softness that did not seek an object.

For years, love had been person-shaped.

It carried names, timelines, unrealized conversations. It lived in the conditional tense: *if I had spoken*, *if she had known*, *if time had turned differently*.

These versions of love were intense but narrow. They required rehearsal. They fed on absence.

This new arrival asked for nothing.

It did not point backwards.

It did not promise forward.

It simply occupied the present with an unfamiliar steadiness.

At first, he mistrusted it.

The mind searched for a cause. Was it memory resurfacing? Suppression lifting? A biochemical shift? The analysis produced hypotheses but no resolution. The sensation persisted regardless.

He noticed that when this state was present, longing lost urgency. Desire remained, but it no longer demanded fulfilment to justify itself.

Love, he realised, had been confused with attachment.

Attachment narrowed attention around a single outcome. Love, in its unbound form, widened perception. It allowed appreciation without ownership, intimacy without claim.

This recognition altered how past relationships appeared.

The first love from childhood no longer felt incomplete. It felt exact. It had existed within the limits available at that time—silence included. Its meaning was not reduced by what never happened.

The second love, carried for years without expression, also softened. What once felt like failure revealed itself as fidelity—to feeling, not to outcome.

He understood then that love does not disappear when unspoken.

It changes location.

When confined to a person, it contracts. When released from expectation, it diffuses—becoming quality rather than narrative.

This diffusion did not erase the human need for connection.

He still noticed attraction. Still felt tenderness toward specific people. What changed was the internal pressure to convert feeling into possession.

This allowed a different kind of meeting.

He could sit with someone without scanning for future potential. He could listen without editing himself for acceptance. He could allow affection without strategising permanence.

Love became a mode of attention rather than a transaction.

Loss, viewed through this lens, is also transformed.

Grief was no longer evidence of error. It was proof of contact. The pain did not argue against love; it testified to its depth.

He stopped asking whether love would stay.

The question lost relevance.

What mattered was whether presence was available when love appeared—regardless of duration or form.

In moments of solitude, the faceless love remained.

It was not euphoric. It was grounded. It made ordinary scenes luminous without exaggeration: a street at dusk, a shared silence, the weight of breath settling.

He understood then why so many traditions struggled to describe love accurately.

As soon as it was given a face, it was mistaken for something else.

What he was learning to trust was subtler.

Love, without a face, did not bind him to the past or promise the future.

It anchored him to what was here.

And in that anchoring, he felt—for the first time—that nothing essential was missing.

Chapter - 10 When Experience Cannot Be Explained

There came a point when language failed him.

Not dramatically. Not all at once. It failed quietly, the way a tool fails when applied beyond its design.

Certain experiences resisted description. When he attempted to explain them, the words sounded exaggerated, even to his own ears. When he stayed precise, the meaning vanished.

He learned this through people's reactions.

Some listened politely and changed the subject. Some smiled indulgently. Others laughed—not cruelly, but dismissively, as if humour was the safest response to uncertainty.

He did not blame them.

He recognised the reflex. He had shared it once.

Modern culture rewarded explanation. Experiences that could not be demonstrated, measured, or repeated on demand were treated as psychological noise. Personal meaning was tolerated only if it remained private.

When he spoke of dreams that echoed waking life, or intuitions that preceded events, he watched credibility evaporate.

The experience itself did not weaken.

His confidence in sharing it did.

For a time, he attempted to translate.

He framed experiences as coincidences. He used the language of probability. He softened conclusions. Still, the core resisted transmission. What mattered was not the event, but the internal shift it produced—and that shift could not be outsourced.

He realised then that explanation was often confused with validation.

To explain was to seek permission.

This recognition was uncomfortable.

He had wanted understanding. What he had been seeking, unknowingly, was agreement.

The practice of one consciousness now faced its first serious test.

Could he remain present without being believed?

He experimented with silence.

Not secrecy—restraint.

When asked, he answered simply. When pressed, he clarified without persuasion. When mocked, he observed the impulse to defend and allowed it to pass.

This was not indifference.

It was discipline.

He noticed something unexpected: as the need to convince dissolved, the experiences themselves integrated more fully. They became less extraordinary and more functional—affecting choices, ethics, and attention.

Extraordinary claims, he saw, often isolate the claimant.

Ordinary embodiment connects.

He also began to recognise the cost of premature disclosure.

Some experiences required incubation. Spoken too early, they fragmented. Held too tightly, they stagnated. Timing mattered.

This reframed his understanding of wisdom traditions.

Silence was not concealment. It was maturation.

He stopped measuring truth by reaction.

Instead, he asked quieter questions: Did this experience reduce fear? Did it sharpen compassion? Did it increase responsibility?

If the answer was yes, the explanation became optional.

He also learned to tolerate ambiguity.

Some experiences might never be fully understood—not by others, perhaps not even by himself. The demand for closure belonged to the same impulse that demanded proof.

Reality, he was learning, did not negotiate on those terms.

This did not place him above scepticism.

It placed him inside it.

He respected doubt—especially his own. He questioned interpretations relentlessly. He resisted conclusions that inflated identity.

What remained, after scrutiny, was modest.

A shift in orientation. A change in how attention moved. A quieter relationship with the unknown.

He no longer introduced these changes as revelations.

They appeared as behaviour.

Listening more carefully.

Reacting less defensively.

Choosing restraint where once he would have asserted.

In this way, experience spoke without explanation.

And he began to understand that some truths are not meant to be believed.

They are meant to be lived.

Chapter - 11
Ethics Without Authority

When certainty dissolved, responsibility intensified.

He had once believed ethics required structure—rules, consequences, external supervision. Without them, behavior felt unanchored. Insight challenged this assumption.

As perception changed, there was no voice issuing commands. No authority appeared to certify what was right.

And yet, action mattered more than ever.

He noticed that awareness itself generated a kind of pressure—not coercive, but clarifying. Certain actions felt immediately discordant. Others aligned without effort. This was not intuition in the romantic sense. It was sensitivity.

The absence of authority did not mean the absence of constraint.

It meant constraint had moved inward.

He became attentive to intention. Not the declared intention, but the one that preceded speech—the impulse beneath justification. When action arose from fear, it carried tension. When it arose from clarity, it required less energy.

This was not moral perfection.

Mistakes continued. Harm still occurred, sometimes unintentionally. What changed was the response.

Defensiveness lost its usefulness.

When confronted, he listened before explaining. When wrong, he corrected without dramatising guilt. Accountability became practical rather than performative.

He understood then why authority-based ethics often failed.

They encouraged compliance, not comprehension.

Without an external judge, self-deception became the primary risk. This demanded vigilance. He learned to question motives ruthlessly, especially when actions appeared virtuous.

Goodness, he noticed, could become another form of identity.

He resisted this.

Ethics without authority required humility—the willingness to revise behaviour when evidence changed, to admit uncertainty, to act without applause.

This ethic did not produce heroes.

It produced consistency.

In small choices—how he spoke to service workers, how he handled conflict, how he treated anonymity—integrity revealed itself. Not as righteousness, but as coherence between perception and action.

He also recognised limits.

Clarity did not eliminate systemic injustice. Awareness did not substitute for structural change. Ethics without authority was personal before it was political.

But personal coherence mattered.

It reduced harm locally. It modelled restraint. It prevented the spread of reactivity.

He stopped asking, "*Is this allowed?*"

He began asking, "*Does this increase or reduce unnecessary suffering?*"

The question was imperfect.

It was sufficient.

This ethic did not guarantee approval.

Sometimes it produced loneliness. Sometimes it required refusing an advantage. Sometimes it meant remaining silent where speech would win points.

He accepted these costs.

Authority had once promised certainty.

Clarity offered responsibility.

He chose the latter.

Not as a principle.

As practice.

Chapter - 12
Learning to Die Before Death

The fear of death did not arrive suddenly.

It had always been present, woven quietly into planning, ambition, and avoidance. What changed was visibility.

As attention refined, he noticed how often decisions were shaped by a future self that demanded protection. Rcputation, lcgacy, imagined continuity—these guided action more than he had admitted.

Death was not only biological.

It was psychological.

Each identity he defended carried an expiration date. The effort to preserve them produced tension. When threatened, they reacted.

He began to experiment—not with risk, but with release.

Small deaths first.

Letting a misunderstanding stand without correction. Allowing an opinion to be outdated. Releasing the need to be remembered accurately.

Each act produced discomfort.

Each act also produced space.

He realised that what he feared death was not awareness, but narrative—the story that claimed ownership over experience. Awareness observed endings without collapsing.

This distinction changed everything.

Mortality ceased to feel abstract. It became instructional.

If this moment were complete, what required postponement? If identity were temporary, what demanded defence?

He noticed that urgency decreased as presence increased.

Time loosened its grip.

Future planning continued, but without anxiety. Goals became provisional. Meaning detached from the outcome.

This did not make him passive.

It made him precise.

Energy previously spent on self-preservation is redirected toward engagement. Conversations deepened. Listening sharpened. Appreciation intensified—not because time was scarce, but because it was sufficient.

He also confronted grief differently.

The deaths of others no longer reinforced personal annihilation. They clarified impermanence without negating connection. Love was not invalidated by the ending.

He understood then why traditions spoke of dying before death.

It was not morbidity.

It was a rehearsal for truth.

By allowing identities to end voluntarily, fear lost leverage. What remained was responsiveness—action informed by present conditions rather than imagined permanence.

This did not eliminate sorrow.

It purified it.

Sadness no longer argued against reality. It moved through awareness without resistance.

He stopped asking how long things would last.

He began asking whether he was fully available while they were here.

In this availability, death lost its role as a threat.

It became a boundary.

And boundaries, he learned, give shape—not meaninglessness—to life.

Chapter - 13
A World That Trains Distraction

He began to notice how rarely attention was left alone.

Not only in himself, but everywhere.

Screens interrupted silence before it could settle. Notifications fractured intention mid-thought. Conversations were punctuated by glances toward elsewhere. Even rest was optimized, measured, tracked.

Distraction was no longer accidental.

It was trained.

The world rewarded responsiveness over presence. Speed over depth. Opinion over observation. Attention became currency, harvested and redistributed by systems that benefited from its fragmentation.

This was not a conspiracy.

It was structured.

He saw how easily the mind adapted. How quickly novelty replaced continuity. How discomfort was anaesthetized with stimulation. Suffering did not vanish—it multiplied quietly beneath constant engagement.

In this environment, clarity required effort.

Not a heroic effort.

Consistent refusal.

Refusal to react immediately. Refusal to fill every pause. Refusal to outsource meaning to algorithms designed to predict preference rather than cultivate understanding.

He noticed that distraction altered ethics.

When attention was scattered, responsibility diffused. Harm became abstract. Consequences felt distant. It was easier to comment than to act, easier to judge than to listen.

Presence, by contrast, localised impact.

When fully attentive, actions carried weight. Words mattered. Indifference became uncomfortable.

This explained why distraction was so effective.

It reduced friction.

A distracted society was easier to manage, easier to divide, easier to exhaust. Not because people were unintelligent, but because intelligence without attention lacked integration.

He did not reject technology.

He rejected unconscious use.

Tools were neutral. Habits were not.

He experimented with limits. Fewer inputs. Longer intervals without stimulation. Conversations without devices present. Reading without interruption.

The results were immediate and unsettling.

Boredom surfaced first. Then restlessness. Then, slowly, coherence. Thoughts connected. Feelings clarified. Time expanded.

He realised how much of his earlier anxiety had been informational rather than existential.

The mind, given fewer signals, reorganised itself.

This had social implications.

Presence disrupted polarisation. It made caricatures harder to maintain. Listening long enough revealed complexity, where outrage preferred simplicity.

He saw that many conflicts were not rooted in incompatible values, but in incompatible attention spans.

To stay with difficulty—to resist premature conclusion—was a quiet form of resistance.

Not dramatic.

Effective.

He did not imagine this practice would spread easily.

Distraction was profitable.

But he also saw that attention, once reclaimed, was self-reinforcing. It restored agency. It reconnected cause and effect.

A world that trained distraction depended on forgetting this.

Remembering became an act.

Not nostalgia.

Orientation.

And orientation, he knew now, determined the future more reliably than any prediction.

Chapter - 14
Teaching Without Preaching

He had once imagined teaching as transmission.

Someone knew something. Someone else did not. Knowledge moved in one direction, reinforced by authority and assessment. This model had shaped his early education, and for years he accepted it without question.

But awareness complicated the picture.

What had changed him most had not been instruction. It had been exposure—being near certain questions long enough for them to take root. No one had given him answers that transformed him. What transformed him was permission to remain curious.

This realisation altered how he related to learning.

Especially with children.

When he watched them, he noticed how quickly curiosity was corrected. How often were questions redirected toward usefulness? How silence was interpreted as disengagement rather than incubation.

He began to experiment.

Instead of explaining, he asked.

Instead of correcting immediately, he waited. He allowed confusion to remain unresolved long enough for attention to deepen. Sometimes this produced frustration. Sometimes insight appeared on its own.

He learned that teaching without preaching required trust.

Trust in intelligence. Trust in timing. Trust in the learner's capacity to discover structure without being handed conclusions.

This approach felt inefficient by conventional standards.

But it was durable.

What emerged through inquiry stayed longer. It integrated more fully. The learner did not borrow certainty—they developed orientation.

He noticed this in himself as well.

Whenever he adopted a belief because it sounded convincing, it remained brittle. When understanding arose through observation, it adapted. It survived contradiction.

Teaching, he realised, was less about content and more about atmosphere.

An atmosphere where attention was valued. Where questions were not punished. Where not-knowing was tolerated.

This did not mean abandoning rigour.

On the contrary, it demanded more precision. Questions had to be honest. Listening had to be complete. Feedback had to be grounded in observation rather than opinion.

He also recognised a danger.

Teaching without preaching could become avoidance—an excuse not to take a position. He learned to distinguish openness from vagueness.

When clarity was earned, it could be stated plainly. Without insistence. Without attachment to acceptance.

He began to see education as relational rather than hierarchical.

The teacher was not above the learner. They were slightly ahead in one dimension, and behind in others. Learning moved laterally as often as it moved forward.

This perspective softened authority without eliminating responsibility.

Guidance remained necessary. Boundaries mattered. Structure supported exploration.

But coercion dissolved.

The most effective lessons, he noticed, were embodied.

Children watched behaviour more closely than speech. They learned how adults handled uncertainty, frustration, and disagreement. Consistency mattered more than explanation.

This returned him to a familiar insight.

Questions shape awareness.

The quality of a culture's questions determined the quality of its attention. And attention, he knew now, shaped everything that followed.

Teaching without preaching was not a technique.

It was alignment.

To live the question long enough for others to feel permitted to ask their own.

That, he understood, was how understanding travelled without force.

Chapter - 15
What Remains Unfinished

He once believed understanding would arrive as completion.

A final insight. A stable position. A place where questions would quiet and effort would recede. This expectation had shaped much of his seeking, even when he claimed otherwise.

What he encountered instead was continuity.

Each clarification revealed further complexity. Each resolution exposed another layer of uncertainty. The movement did not end—it refined.

At first, this felt disappointing.

There was no summit. No moment of arrival justified the journey retroactively. What existed was a rhythm: noticing, adjusting, returning.

He came to see that the desire for closure was another form of control.

It sought to freeze understanding into possession.

Life resisted this.

What remained unfinished was not failure.

It was capacity.

The openness to revise. The willingness to remain responsive. The humility to accept that perception would always be partial.

He noticed how quickly certainty hardened into identity. How answers, once defended, lost their usefulness. He learned to hold conclusions lightly—not as provisional truths to be discarded, but as tools subject to context.

This stance did not weaken conviction.

It stabilised it.

He could act decisively without pretending permanence. He could commit without demanding that commitment define him forever.

Unfinishedness also altered his relationship with others.

He no longer expected agreement to validate understanding. The difference became informative rather than threatening. Conversations extended rather than concluded.

This did not eliminate conflict.

It reframed it.

Conflict signalled misalignment of attention, not a moral defect. Repair mattered more than victory. Continuity mattered more than being right.

He also learned to forgive incompleteness in himself.

Some fears persisted. Certain patterns softened slowly. Old reflexes resurfaced under pressure. None of this negated the work.

Progress, he understood, was not linear.

It spiralled.

Returning to familiar questions with altered perception was not repetition—it was deepening.

The unfinished carried an ethical dimension.

It prevented the final authority. It resisted dogma. It left room for others to enter without submission.

This, he realised, was the quiet responsibility of awareness—to remain open without becoming diffuse, grounded without becoming rigid.

He stopped asking what the book would conclude.

He began asking what it would invite.

If it had invited attention rather than belief, patience rather than urgency, responsibility rather than reassurance, it would have served its purpose.

The story did not close.

It continued wherever attention was practised.

In classrooms. In conversations. In moments of loss. In ordinary decisions made without witnesses.

What remained unfinished was not a problem to solve.

It was a way of being.

And he understood, finally, that to remain unfinished was not to lack direction.

It was to stay alive.

After Ending

For a long time, I searched for meaning as if it were hidden somewhere else—in dreams, in love, in insight.

Eventually, I noticed something simpler.

The moments that changed me most were not dramatic. They did not announce themselves. They arrived quietly, often disguised as hesitation, silence, or unfinished feeling.

Nothing in this book proves anything.

It only points to a way of paying attention that does not divide experience into higher and lower, real and unreal, important and trivial.

If there is unity, it does not need to be achieved.

It only needs to be noticed.

This story does not conclude.

It pauses.

What continues cannot be written without turning experience into explanation, and explanation into distance.

So, I leave it here—

not as an answer,

But as an invitation

to notice what remains when attention stays.